Through the Rainbow

Violet Book 3

Simon's Book

by E. S. BRADBURNE

Illustrated by PAMELA MARA

SCHOFIELD & SIMS LTD., HUDDERSFIELD

Simon is at school. He is making a book.
It is a book all about him.
It says

This is a book about me.
I am Simon.
I am seven.
It is my birthday today.

I am seven years old today.
Today is my birthday.
Elizabeth is 5 years old.
My baby is one month old.
Spot is 3 years old.
Spot is not a puppy now, he is a big dog.
I play with my baby.
I take him for a walk.
Elizabeth and I take him for a walk
in the park with mummy.
He is a good baby.

This is my mummy
and this is my daddy.
Here is Elizabeth, she is my sister.
Here is my baby.
This is my dog, Spot, and my cat.
This is all my family.
I help my mummy in the house.
I help to wash the dishes
and I help my daddy in the garden.
I help him to weed the garden.

This is my friend, Peter.
I like Peter. He is my best friend.
He has a sister too.
Peter and his sister live in the house
opposite to me.
Peter has a puppy and a model aeroplane.
It is a black puppy.
I go to play with my friend Peter
in his garden.
I can play with his model aeroplane.
We play in the front garden
and we play in the back garden.
We are going to play
in his garden today.
Peter is six years old
and his sister is seven years old.

Today is my birthday
and I am going to have a party.
Peter is coming to my party
and his sister is coming too.
We will have some buns and a big cake.
There will be candles on the cake.
There will be seven candles,
seven white candles.
I will light the candles
on my birthday cake.
I will light all the seven candles
when I have my birthday party.
Daddy and mummy gave me a new train
for my birthday. It has a silver engine
and six yellow coaches. It can go fast.
I am going to play with it after school.
Daddy made me a station for my train.
I like having a birthday.
I would like to have a birthday
every day.
I would like to have a cake
with candles on it every day.

14

Here is my house. I live at number 2.
We all live in this house.
It is at the end of the street.
I have a garden at the front of my house
and a garden at the back
and a garden at the side.
This is the house I made in my garden.
I have made a house in a tree too.
My friend Peter and I play in my garden
and we play in the park.
There is a pond in the park.
I sail my boat on it.
There are some ducks on the pond.
Elizabeth and I give them buns and cake
to eat.
I give them some every day.

Next month
we are all going for a holiday.
We are going to the country.
We are going for a month.
I like going to the country.
We can play in the fields
and go in the wood.
There is a big wood and a river.
There is a good tree to climb
in the wood.
It is a great big tree and I can climb
right to the top.
Elizabeth and I paddle in the river.
We catch tadpoles and tiddlers
and take them home.
I can catch the tadpoles with my hand.
We look for eggs in the wood.
We do not take the eggs,
we do not even feel them.
We will be in the country
all next month.

I like going to the country
and I like going to the seaside.
I like making a castle in the sand.
I like to make a great big castle
with a moat round it
and I like to climb up the rocks.
I like to see the gulls
and look for their eggs.
I can sail my boat on the sea
and I can paddle.
I like a holiday in the country
and I like a holiday by the sea too.
I would like to have a month
in the country
and a month by the sea.
It would be a long holiday.
It would be good.
I would like to live in the country.
I would like to live there
for years and years and years.

I have black hair and brown eyes.
My sister has brown eyes too.
Elizabeth's hair is not black,
it is yellow.
She has long yellow hair.
It is very light yellow.
My friend Peter has brown hair.
My baby has no hair at all.

Here is my coat and my hat.
Here are my shoes and socks.
My coat is brown. It is a light brown,
and my shoes are black.
It is my best coat.
This is my vest and shirt.
My vest is white.
Mummy says I make my shirt black,
then she has to wash it.
She has to wash my vest too.

I have a new vest and a new shirt.
It is a yellow shirt with a zip.
I can do up the zip myself.
I like my new shirt.
Mummy made it for me.
She put the zip in it.
Mummy is good at making clothes.
She can make socks for daddy.
She can knit them with wool.
Elizabeth can knit too.
Mummy made a coat for my sister.
It has a zip in the front.
Mummy made all the clothes
for my baby.

This is my hand.
It is my left hand.
I can measure it.
It is 10 centimetres long.
There are 5 fingers on my left hand.
I can draw round my hand.
I can draw round all the fingers.

This is my right hand.
I can measure it.
It is 10 centimetres long too.
I write with my right hand.
Some people write with their left hand.
There are 5 fingers on my right hand
and 5 fingers on my left hand.
I have 10 fingers.
My daddy has 10 fingers
and my mummy has 10 fingers.
Elizabeth has 10 fingers
and my baby has 10 fingers.
Daddy and mummy
and Elizabeth and my baby and me,
we have 50 fingers.

I can measure my feet.
This is my left foot.
I can draw round it
and I can measure it.
My left foot is 18 centimetres long.

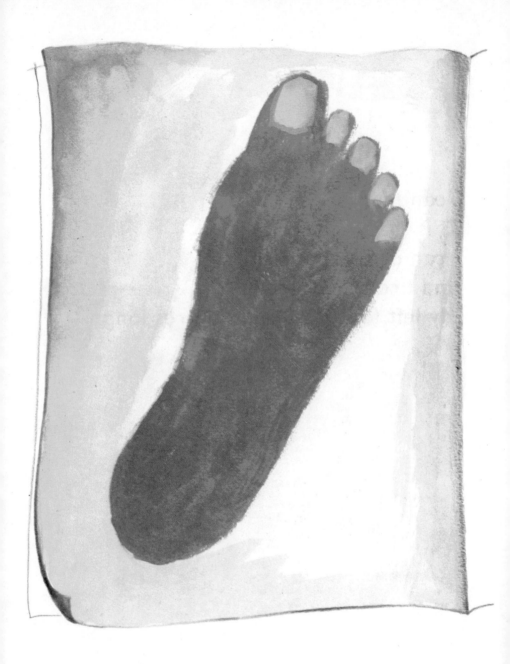

This is my right foot.
I can measure it too.
I can draw round my foot
and measure it.
My right foot is 18 centimetres long.
I can measure Elizabeth's foot too.
It is 15 centimetres long.
I can draw round daddy's feet
and measure them too.
Daddy's feet are very big.

I can measure myself
and I can measure all my family.
I am one metre 30 centimetres tall.
My daddy is one metre 80 centimetres tall.
My mummy is one metre 65 centimetres
tall.
Elizabeth is one metre 20 centimetres tall.
My baby is 50 centimetres long.
He is very little,
and Elizabeth's doll is 20 centimetres
long.

I can weigh myself
and I can weigh all my family.
I weigh 25 kilos.
I can weigh Elizabeth.
She is 20 kilos.
I can weigh mummy.
She is 56 kilos,
and I can weigh daddy.
He is 75 kilos.
My baby is 4 kilos.
He is very light.
My daddy is not light.

I can jump and run.
I can jump 60 centimetres.
I can run fast.
I am good at running.
I am good at throwing and catching.
I can jump on one foot.
I can jump on 2 feet.
I can climb a tree.
I can draw pictures and paint them.
I like to draw pictures.
I like to write a story
and draw pictures to go with it.
I like to make a train or a boat
out of wood
and I like to make a man
out of clay.

Here is my bed.
It is at the back of the house.
I can see into the garden
from my window.
I go up the stairs to bed.
I go up 10 stairs.
I take off my clothes.
I take off my shirt first.
I take off my yellow shirt with the zip.
Then I take off my new white vest
and put myself to bed.
I put my vest and shirt
at the foot of the bed.
I put all my clothes
at the foot of the bed.
I put them all tidy when I go to bed.
I read to myself in bed
and then I turn off the light.
The light is over my bed.
I can turn it off myself.

Every day I get up
and put on my clothes.
I wash myself.
I put on my white vest first,
then my yellow shirt with a zip.
I do up the zip myself.
I look in the mirror and do my hair.
Then I go down stairs to have breakfast.
I go down 10 stairs.
If I am in a hurry I jump
down the stairs.
Mummy does not like me to jump
down the stairs.
She says,
Simon, you are not to jump down the stairs.
You are to walk. Then I walk down.
My friend Peter and I
like to play on the stairs.
We climb up to the top
and then we jump down.
We hide under the stairs
when we play hide and seek.

I have breakfast with mummy and daddy
and Elizabeth.
I have breakfast with them every day.
My baby has breakfast with us too.
We have eggs and tea for breakfast.
I like brown eggs for my breakfast.
When I have finished breakfast
I go to school.
I go to school on a bus.
I go on the bus every school day.
It is not far to school on the bus.
I like to go on the top deck
and I like to be at the front,
then I can see out of the window.
I see my friend Peter on the bus.
He and his sister come on the bus
with Elizabeth and me.

This is my teacher.
I like my teacher.
I am learning to read at school.
I read to my teacher every day.
This is me reading to her.
I have read 20 books.
I work very hard at school.

This is my table at school.
I can measure it.
It is 90 centimetres long.
I am working at my table.
We are all working hard.
I can count and write numbers.
I can write odd and even numbers.
Here are some of the numbers I can write.

2   5   12   6   20

I can draw squares and circles
and I can weigh and measure.
I can write a story.
I have made a book
with a long story in it.
It is about an aeroplane
and it has pictures in it.
They are very good pictures.
I finished my book today
and I am going to give it
to my daddy.

Here are the children at my school.
They are singing.
I like singing.
After singing we have dinner.
I have dinner with the children.
I like school dinner.
I like the cook at my school.
When we have finished dinner
we go out to play.
We go out to play every day.
I like being at school.
I like learning to read and write.

Here are the children playing at my school.
We are all playing catching.
I am running after the children.
You can see me playing
with my friend Peter.
I am good at running and catching.
We play hide and seek.
We jump on one foot
and we jump on 2 feet.
We play at being a train,
and we play giants and fairies,
and we play ball.
I play at being an aeroplane.

After school is over
I go home on the bus.
It is a red bus with six wheels.
We all go up on the top of the bus.
Peter and his sister
and Elizabeth and her friend,
we all go on the bus.
Then, when we get home,
we all play in the park
at the end of the street.
We take the dog with us
and we take a ball.
Peter and I climb a tree.
We climb a great tall tree.
Then we all go home for tea.

After tea I help mummy
to wash the dishes.
I put them all away.
Then mummy will read us a story.
I like a story about a tiger
and a story about an aeroplane.
After mummy has read to us
we have to go to bed.
Mummy has to put Elizabeth to bed
and I can put myself to bed.
I take off my yellow shirt
and my new white vest
and then I get into bed.
Mummy has to put my baby to bed.
She has to wash him.
I wash myself.
Mummy does not help me.
When I am in bed
daddy will come to read me a story,
or else I read to myself.
Then I put out the light
and it is the end of the day.

Can you make a book about yourself,
like Simon did?
Can you draw some pictures in it?
Tell how old you are
and how tall you are.
Can you measure and weigh yourself?
How tall are you? Are you one metre tall?
What do you weigh?
Do you weigh 25 kilos?
Can you measure your foot and your hand?
How long are they?
Have you got black hair and brown eyes
like Simon,
or yellow hair and brown eyes,
like Elizabeth?
Write about your house
and your garden.
Write about all your family.
Count the fingers in your family
and then count the feet.

Have you a sister? How old is she?
Has she got yellow hair or black hair?
Has she got brown eyes?
Can you measure her? How tall is she?
Have you a baby? Does it weigh 4 kilos?
How old is your baby?
Is it a month old?
Have you a best friend?
Write about your clothes.
Tell about your coat and hat.
Are they red or brown or yellow?
Write about what you have to eat.
Tell about your dinner
and your breakfast and your tea.
What do you have to eat for dinner
and what do you have for breakfast?